Night
Journey

by Lynn Cullen

illustrated by Paul Tong

MODERN CURRICULUM PRESS

Pearson Learning Group

Babies don't wait until morning to be born. That is why I drive the dark streets.

The drugstore, the movie theater, and the grocery are all dark. I wait alone at the stoplight. Red changes to green. I start up again.

A cat crosses the road in front of me. I watch her slip off into the shadows. We are the only ones awake, the cat and I. The rest of the world sleeps.

I too was sleeping until my pager began to beep. But a certified nurse midwife does not turn over and return to sleep—not even when she is tired. Once a baby has begun its journey into life, a nurse midwife must be there.

I pat the pager hooked to my belt. It is a very valued possession. It lets me know if an expectant mother has worries. It warns me if troubles arise. To me, it seems to sing when a baby is on the way.

I imagine how midwives were called before the days of phones and pagers.

I picture a husband on horseback. He is reckless with worry as he gallops to the midwife's home.

"My wife's time has come!" he cries to the midwife. "Come quickly!"

I see a girl running barefoot through the winter night. The streets of her city are crowded with darkened buildings. She is near tears as she looks from side to side.

"Is this the midwife's street?" she asks. "I don't know which is her house, and Mama needs her now."

I sigh with relief as I imagine kindly neighbors taking her to the midwife's door.

Midwives have always been needed. For as long as babies have come into this world, we have been there.

In early times, we relied on instinct, herbs, and hard-won experience.

Now we are trained and certified, full of scientific knowledge. We are friends of medicine and doctors.

Throughout the ages, we have learned our work because we love it. We love to help mothers deliver their babies. We are experts on the journey into life.

I turn my car toward the bright lights of the hospital parking lot. Here, neither moon nor sun rules the hours. Even at night, the hospital is a hive of activity. Its workers wear suits of blue, green, or white.

I check in at the desk. Nearby, a surgeon in green goes over the details of an operation with a doctor in white.

I am told that the baby will come soon. I put on my own blue suit, for it is time to go to work.

It is morning when at last I leave the mother. She is filled with emotion as she gazes into her newborn daughter's eyes. She has never loved a possession the way she loves this baby.

The baby grabs her mother's finger with her tiny red hand.

I slip out, unnoticed. My work is finished.

The streets are filling up now. Men and women sit behind the wheels of their cars. Some of them sip coffee at stoplights. Dogs are being taken for their morning walks.

My cat friend has disappeared. Perhaps she is curled up in a chair inside a warm house, deep in sleep. Not I.

Soon I will drive to my office. I have a full day of appointments ahead of me. My work is not just greeting babies as they are born. Modern technology allows me to help them long before that day.

Indeed, teaching a mother how to care for her unborn baby is an important part of my job. I help her make sensible choices and take care of herself. An expectant mother cannot be reckless. A midwife's work is to make the journey into life safer for both mother and child.

My eyes are weary. My back aches. Still, I shake off my pains. I must concentrate on the road. I must think of what is yet to come. I have my own journey to make.

But I do not drive to my office just yet.

At home, I find my children sleeping in their beds. I take the time to kiss each of them gently, to smooth their rumpled hair. I let them wake and find the love in my eyes.

For birth is only the beginning of the journey of life. The rest is lived each day.